W9-BZB-096

Off to Kindergarten

By Tony Johnston • Illustrated by Melissa Sweet

Cartwheel
B·O·O·K·S®

SCHOLASTIC INC

New York   Toronto   London   Auckland   Sydney
Mexico City   New Delhi   Hong Kong   Buenos Aires

I'm off to kindergarten now.
I'd better take my bear.
He likes to sit beside me, so
I'll take a little chair.

A pillow will be handy, too,
in case we need a nap,
so we will not be cranky-heads.
(There's nothing worse than that.)

I'll pack a cookie for myself,
one for my teacher, too,
and one for all my brand-new friends.
(Or maybe even two!)

I'll lug a lot of milk along
in case we get all dry
from gobbling all those cookies down
and shrivel up—oh, my!

I've *got* to have some books to read
while I enjoy my snack.
I'll pile mine up like pancakes, then
I'll pull the wobbly stack.

I can't forget to take my mud.
(I'll write it on a list.)
For mud's what everybody loves
to muish and guish and squish.

I'm going to bring my easel and
my paints to paint a tree
with giant smelly flowers for
a giant bumblebee.

I'll take my backhoe with a scoop
to dig holes dirtily.
I'll bring some moles along because
moles like to dig like me.

My robot has to come to school.
His name is Techno-Tim.

He walks around as stiff as starch.
(And I can walk like him.)

I guess I'll need my sandbox so
that I can make a fort
to crawl inside with all my friends
and jump in and cavort.

I need a bunch of nice clean clothes
for when I'm caked with sand.
'Cause otherwise I'll itch all day,
and itching is not grand.

Oh, gosh! I nearly left behind
my super set of swings.
I'll swoop the kindergarten sky
and soar like I have wings.

I think I'd better get a truck
to haul my stuff to school,
and moving men to load it up.
(I'll give them cookies, too.)

My mother says, "You don't need all
these things, my little Bill.
Your teacher will have everything."
"She will?" I ask. "She will."

I leave my piles of stuff at home.
I sing out, "Doodle-eeeee!"
I'm off to kindergarten now.
And all I take is—ME!

For brand-new kindergartners everywhere — T.J.

To Azalea — M.S.

Text copyright © 2007 by Roger D. Johnston and Susan T. Johnston, as Trustees
of the Johnston Family Trust. Illustrations copyright © 2007 by Melissa Sweet.

Library of Congress Cataloging-in-Publication Data

Johnston, Tony, 1942-
Off to kindergarten / by Tony Johnston ; illustrated by Melissa Sweet.
p. cm.
Summary: A young boy lists all the things he will have to take with
him on his first day in kindergarten.
ISBN 0-439-73090-2
[1. Kindergarten--Fiction. 2. First day of school--Fiction. 3. Schools--Fiction.
4. Stories in rhyme.] I. Sweet, Melissa, ill. II. Title.

PZ8.3.J639Off 2007   [E]--dc22   2006023429

ISBN-13: 978-0-439-73090-7
ISBN-10: 0-439-73090-2
10 9 8 7 6 5 4 3 2 1   7 8 9 10 11/0
Printed in Singapore
First printing, July 2007

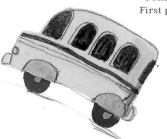
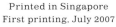